ABOUT THE AUTHOR

Swapna Haddow lives in New Zealand with her son, her husband and Archie the dog. She spends her time writing, eating cake and making sure her son doesn't flatten her husband as he attempts to master his human cannonball trick.

ABOUT THE ILLUSTRATOR

Sheena Dempsey is a children's author and illustrator. She loves to draw animals, from dirty rats to mean cats and heroic pigeons, too. She lives in Folkstone with her partner, Mick, and their greyhound, Sandy.

DAVE Pigeon (Royal Coo!)

Dave Pigeon's book on How to Escape a Coup in the Coop

Typed up by Skipper
instead of **Swapna Haddow**
who was busy telling everyone she once
used the toilet at Windsor Castle

Illustrated by
Sheena Dempsey,
who once used the toilet at
Reigate Library

90 YEARS OF EXCELLENCE
FABER & FABER

First published in 2019
by Faber and Faber Limited
Bloomsbury House
74–77 Great Russell Street
London WC1B 3DA

Designed by Faber and Faber
Printed and bound in the UK by
CPI Group (UK) Ltd, Croydon, CR0 4YY

A CIP record for this book is available from the British Library

ISBN/978-0-571-33698-2

2 4 6 8 10 9 7 5 3 1

For Archie – SH
For Sandy – SD

The Royal Family

invites you to celebrate the arrival

of the Royal Baby

You are all requested to attend a fahncy party
at the palace to feast on scrumptious patisserie
and delectable confectionery baked by Chef Chocolat
Poulet, the official bakers to the Royal Family

MENU

Exquisite marzipan figs

Mouth-watering passion fruit meringues

Dreamy strawberry marshmallows

Chocolate éclairs, custard éclairs,

pistachio éclairs, sticky maple éclairs,

red-velvet-pulled-pork-salted-caramel éclairs

(basically all the éclairs)

Honeyed raspberry tartlets

Warmed jammy sable biscuits

Sugary buttermilk doughnuts

Fizzy orange popping-candy popcorn

(a Royal Family favourite)

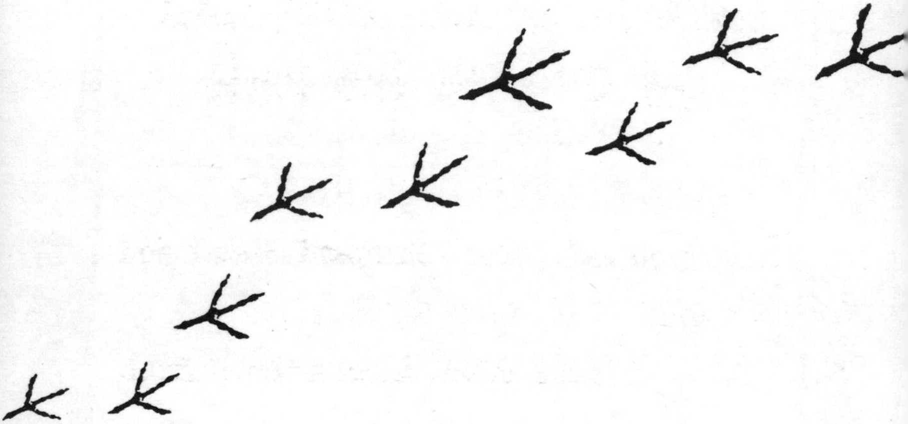

1

Dave Is Up with the Lark and Off to the Park

'Have you seen this, Skipper? Have you *seen* this?'

Dave whipped out a sheet of card from his sling. The card was decorated in gold ink and swirly writing and now jam and crumbs from being stuffed in the same place my best friend stashed his biscuit snacks.

Through the blur of Dave's flapping

feathers as he waved the card under my beak, I could just about read it was an invitation for a party at the Royal Human Palace.

'It's an invitation for a party that happened *yesterday*, Dave,' I said.

'Exactly,' Dave said with a wide grin.

It's funny what you remember when you look back to the start of a day that turned into a claw-screech of a disaster. I remember the sun was shining. The clouds were as cottony as a baby squab wrapped in candyfloss. And it was wonderfully peaceful.

I should've known it was the sort of day that Dave would ruin with a catbrained plan.

Dave had hopped off to the park early to have a gossip with the other birds. He'd come back to the shed less than ten minutes later, all excited and fluffed up, with the golden invitation.

'Skipper, I have some pigeontastic news!'

'Did you find the stash of biscuits I'd been saving to have as a midnight snack?' I asked, hunting in my usual hiding spot.

'Yes, Skipper. I ate those ages ago.'

'But they were mine!'

'They were very tasty,' Dave said, a grin stretched across his beak as he remembered chowing down on *my* biscuits. 'You should really change where you hide your snacks.'

He bobbed across the ledge of our well-loved shed and jumped up on to the lid of a paint can. 'I know where we can find the most delicious gooey stale snacks you have ever eaten.'

Gooey and stale? That was almost unheard of.

'Where?' I asked, suspicious but very aware of the loud grumbling in my tummy.

That's when he showed me the fancy invitation and explained his plan.

The park pigeons told Dave that there had been a party at the Human Palace the previous day. Parties meant only one thing. Full bins. And royal parties meant only one thing. Full royal bins. The royal black bags and golden wheelie bins would be full to bursting with popcorn, sweet delights and biscuits. Not to mention half-eaten marshmallows and sticky meringue crumbs. There was even a rumour that there were the biscuits with the jam in the middle. My favourites.

'Those park pigeons know all the bins to visit for the best treats,' Dave squawked excitedly.

OK. So you know how I said on page two that Dave's plan would be catbrained? It turns out that once in a while he does have a pigeontastic idea, and this was it!

Hey! Sometimes I have a pigeontastic idea twice in a while.

He really doesn't.

We were going to the Human Palace! I couldn't wait. I remembered tales of the Human Palace my granny told Dave and me when we were just tiny squabs. She spoke of gold-plated iron gates, where the bars were perfectly placed and perfectly sized for a pigeon to squeeze through. She'd heard of a huge fountain outside where pigeons could bathe and drink water, and when she spoke of the glorious Mall, made for pigeons to run free and fly, her head would tilt to the side and her eyes would get misty as she imagined herself gliding down towards the palace, the wind in her wings.

Your granny never glided anywhere. She mainly farted, Skipper.

Dave! I was setting a lovely scene there.

It's true though. When I think of Granny, I think of farts. She really was a champion farter.

Do you remember when she actually won the Pigeon Farting Championships?

I remember. She almost blew a branch off a tree.

There was no time to waste. Gourmet snacks were on offer and my feathers were all a-jitter with excitement for my first trip to the Human Palace.

'Quick, Dave,' I cried. 'Let's get your prosthetic wing on.'

'There's no time,' Dave said, already halfway to the shed door. 'It's so fiddly and we can't let a single other pigeon get to the palace before us.'

So we waddled off to the nearest train station and caught the first train to the city centre.

The Humans, as always, seemed very amused by pigeons on the train and clicked on their cameras, taking pictures of Dave and me, which Dave happily blew out his chest feathers for. A Little Human fed me soggy rice cake bits as his mum dozed—

Rice cakes? You had rice cakes? And YOU DIDN'T TELL ME.

You could've had some but you were too busy posing.

Harrumph. I can't help it if my fans want pictures of me, Skipper. I have a very important job starring in all these books you keep writing.

As I was saying, a Little Human fed me soggy rice cake bits as his mum dozed, and it was only after Dave had struck his one pillionth pose that we finally reached the stop for the Royal Human Palace.

'I bet I could be a prince,' Dave said, as we jumped off the train on to the platform. 'I've always thought I had the feathers for it.'

'Why would you want to be a prince?' I asked, as we dodged hundreds of Human ankles and looked for signs leading to the Human Palace.

'I could lie around all day eating excellent snacks.'

'I'm not sure that's *all* they do,' I said, as we followed a trail of sticky orange popcorn along the pavement. 'Besides, isn't that what you do anyway?'

'Skipper, I work very hard—' Dave stopped so suddenly, I tripped over his claws and fell beak first into a lamppost.

'Dave!' I said, scrambling to my feet and rubbing my bruised beak.

'Skipper,' Dave said, not even offering me a wing up. 'You know that pigeontastic plan I had to get to the palace before the other pigeons?'

'Yes?'

My friend stared straight ahead of us, his eyes wide and his lower beak hanging open. I followed his gaze.

We weren't the only ones who had heard about the royal bins.

A mammoth crowd of grey-feathered bodies and pink claws blocked our way to the golden gates. When I say 'mammoth', I mean think of a number, times it by a gajillion-bazillion, add on an extra wajillion-cabillion, minus one, and that was how many birds we were looking at.

'Where did all these pigeons come from?' Dave shouted, as we pushed our way forward, only to be trampled and nudged aside by the colossal swarm of bird bottoms.

'Isn't that your dad over there?' I yelled back over the racket of coos and caws. I pointed my wing at a pigeon shoving his way through the throng of birds, straight towards a scrap of pitta bread.

'Dad,' Dave screeched, jumping up on to my shoulders.

DAD!

Dave's dad, the legendary racing pigeon Mickey Lightning, whirled round and

grinned at us, a nubbin of salivary pitta hanging from his beak. 'Boys!' he cried. 'Isn't this great?'

'Hi, Mickey,' I called, waving back. 'Can you get us in?'

Dave wobbled, pushing his foot into my eye. 'We can't get to the gates.'

'It's packed over here and the food is running out,' Mickey cawed. 'I'm sure there are more snacks around the back.'

We heaved our way through the throng of pigeons and followed the path, lined with bunting, around the side of the palace towards the back. Our stomachs ached as we watched the mass of birds feasting on sweets and biscuits.

'This is hopeless,' Dave wailed.

'What's hopeless?' came a voice.

Looking up, I saw a hole in the iron side gate, where rust had crumbled the metal. A pigeon's head poked through and stared at us.

My lower beak dropped open. I reached out with a wing to make sure Dave was next to me. He was.

But what didn't make any sense at all was the face looking back at me through the gate.

It was Dave!

2
We're as Dead as the Dodos

Well, not quite Dave.

The pigeon squeezed out of the hole in the gate and shook his feathers.

I looked at Dave. I looked at the pigeon. I looked back at Dave. Dave looked at the pigeon. He looked at me. He looked back at the pigeon. The pigeon looked at Dave. He looked at me. He looked back at Dave. Dave looked down at his feathery tummy. Then he looked back up at the pigeon.

My head bobbed from Dave to the pigeon

and back to Dave again. The resemblance was uncanny. They looked so similar, they could have been brothers. They could've been twins.

'Dave,' I said. 'This pigeon looks just like you!'

'I'm not "Dave",' the pigeon said, straightening a lustrous purple velvet robe that flowed over his back and wings. 'I'm Prince Raju.'

It was the Royal Pigeon. The actual Royal Pigeon! 'Dave,' I hissed. 'That's the actual Royal Pigeon!'

He flapped me quiet, slapping his good wing over my beak.

'Are you a mirror?' Dave whispered, his eyes wide with shock as he peered at the prince.

'No, I'm not a mirror,' Prince Raju said indignantly. 'And why do you have my face?'

'Why do you have *my* face?' Dave said.

'Give me back my face,' Prince Raju shrieked.

'Give me back *my* face,' Dave squawked back.

Both pigeons turned to me.

'Well?' Prince Raju squawked. 'Who has whose face?'

I looked the pigeons up and down. It was hard to tell them apart. They had similar bodies, similar claws and a similar patchy tail of feathers.

'You're almost identical!' I said slowly.

'That's so pigeonist of you, Skipper,' Dave said, all huffy and fluffy. 'Not all pigeons look the same. Next you'll be saying I look like you. Or that pigeon flying past us.'

Both Dave and Prince Raju stared up at the pigeon flying overhead and then turned back to glare at me.

'Of course pigeons look completely different from each other,' I said, holding up my wings. 'It's just that you two look VERY similar.'

'He's right,' Prince Raju said, looking Dave up and down. 'You do look a lot like me and that's a very handsome face you have.'

'I think you mean *you* look a lot like *me*,' Dave said back. He nodded at the prince with a smile. 'You do have a handsome face, almost as handsome as mine.'

'Prince Raju? Prince Raju?' came a coo from across the gate.

'Oh crumbs,' the prince said, his shoulders dropping. 'That's Kapi.'

'Who's Kapi?' I asked.

'I'm Kapi.' A tall skinny pigeon with a long neck hopped through the hole. He peered down his beak at Dave and me before turning to the prince. 'Are these

pigeons bothering
you, Sire?'

'Not at all, Kapi,'
Prince Raju said. 'In
fact we were just talking
about how similar myself and Dave look.'

Kapi looked at Dave. He looked at Prince
Raju. He looked back at Dave. Dave looked
at Kapi. He looked at Prince Raju. He looked
back at Kapi. Kapi looked at Dave again.
He looked at Prince Raju again. He looked
back at Dave again. Dave looked down at
his feathery tummy. Then he looked back
up at Kapi.

'Sire!' Kapi squawked at Prince
Raju. 'Can't you see this is an imposter
pretending to be you?'

I took a step towards Prince Raju and Kapi. 'I think you are a little confused,' I said. 'Dave just happens to look like Prince Raju. He's not an imposter.'

'GUARDS!' Kapi screamed.

'What's this guy's problem?' Dave asked.

'Oh no, oh no, oh no,' Prince Raju said, ignoring Dave. He flapped his wings in panic and his purple robe twisted around his body. 'Kapi! This is all getting out of hand.'

'GUARDS!' Kapi shouted again. 'Take these insolent pigeons away!'

Two ravens jumped over the gate and launched towards Dave and me on Kapi's command. Before we could even flap our wings, the birds grabbed us by our tail feathers and pushed us through the hole and into the palace courtyard.

'What's going on?' Dave panicked.

'I don't know,' I said, unable to hide the wobble in my voice.

'You are being arrested for stealing the Royal Pigeon's face,' Kapi screeched at Dave, before the raven guards shoved us forward.

I could feel the heavy breath of the ravens on my neck as they rammed me and Dave across the courtyard.

'Stop dragging your claws,' one of the guards hooted at us as we were marched towards a cobblestone tower.

I arched my head round and came beak to beak with him. 'Where are we going?'

'To the dungeon,' the slick black bird snarled at us.

Dave and me were shoved through the dark opening of the tower. The cobblestone walls were shadowy and cold, lit only by a small stream of light from a tiny window.

In the corner were two crates, with the letters 'W I N E' stamped on the side. They were stacked one on top of the other to create a wooden cage.

'MOVE,' the bigger of the ravens said, pushing me and Dave towards the cage.

Both ravens twisted their curved beaks into a metal fastening that held the crates together. One of the ravens raised the top crate with his beak while the other tossed me and Dave in, beak first.

'What's going to happen to us?' Dave bawled.

'You two are going to spend a long, LONG time in jail.'

'What?!' I sobbed, my body trembling as I clung to Dave on the cold wooden floor. 'Why?'

'As ordered by the valet for the Royal Pigeon for stealing the prince's face,' the raven crowed, as the top crate slammed down with a bang and the metal fastening pinged into place.

And then there was silence.

3

I'm Stark Raven Mad

'What are we going to do? What are we going to do? What are we going to do?'

I'd asked myself the same question a gazillion times, as I paced the tiny length of the prison cell.

There was no way out. The crate was sealed shut from the outside. And our feathered bodies were too large to slip through the gaps between the wooden slats.

Dave let out a moan as he continued

blubbering in a heap of salty tears and feathers.

'My life is over—'

'Shhh,' I hissed at him.

I could hear a faint tapping on the ground.

'Don't tell me to shush,' Dave wept. 'My life is over—'

'Shhhh!'

'Why are you being so mean, Skipper?'

'Can you hear that?'

Dave stopped crying.

There it was again. It was the sound of claws on stone.

'Someone's coming, Dave,' I whispered, hugging him close. 'Maybe we're going to be saved!'

The clatter of claws got louder and louder. Dave and me stood, brushing down our feathers.

It was the prince and his guards!

'Prince Raju—' I started.

'Do not address the Royal Pigeon unless you have been invited to,' one of the ravens screeched.

'That's quite enough, Corvus,' Prince Raju said, holding up a wing at the guard. 'Sorry about that, old sport,' he said, turning to me. 'Corvus may seem like a brute but he's a big softy really.'

There was nothing soft about Corvus, who, by the way, was still glaring at us. He was about as soft as a brick wrapped in another brick, wrapped in a brick.

'Prince Raju,' I started again. 'I think there has been a mix-up—'

'Why have we been sent to jail?' Dave howled.

'I'm so sorry,' the prince replied. 'My valet, Kapi, is rather overprotective. This is all a terrible mistake.'

'So we don't have to spend the rest of our lives in this crate?' Dave asked hopefully.

'Who said you would?' the prince exclaimed.

'Your guard,' I said, pointing towards the raven.

'Oh, Corvus,' the prince chuckled. 'You are funny.'

There was nothing funny about Corvus. He was about as funny as a brick wrapped

in another brick, wrapped in a brick.

I helped Dave to his feet as he dried his eyes on his sling.

I think you are making far too much of this crying business, Skipper.

Dave, you were crying like a baby squab.

I wasn't crying like a baby. I was crying like a respectable pigeon.

This is a picture of a crying baby and a crying Dave. Spot the difference.

'Let them out immediately,' the prince ordered, signalling to Corvus to unlock the crate.

Corvus pulled us out of the wooden cage and we followed the prince out of the tower, back into the courtyard. The sky felt so bright I had to squeeze my eyes shut for a moment as we left the dark dungeon.

'I apologise for that misunderstanding,' Prince Raju said. 'Kapi can be a little overzealous.'

'And where is this Kapi now?' Dave asked, arching his head left and right to scour the yard for the prince's valet.

'I sent him away for the moment so we could talk,' the prince replied. 'He is very sorry.'

I had a feeling that Kapi wasn't that sorry.

'Right, well, we'll be off,' Dave said, turning on his heel. 'We came here for snacks, not to be thrown in jail.'

Dave grabbed my wing and charged towards the gate.

'Wait!' the prince called after us. 'I can get you food.'

Dave whirled back on his heel, spinning me round like a carousel.

'What kind of food?' he asked.

It didn't really matter what the prince offered. I knew Dave was as hungry as I was and if Prince Raju served up a rotten tomato we would've gobbled it down.

Rotten tomatoes go very well with stinky cheese. Write that down, Skipper. You'll need it when you write my cookbook.

'I can offer you the best royal snacks in town,' the prince said with a grin.

'I am truly very sorry about how you were treated.' He offered us a wing of friendship. 'I hope we can be friends.'

'Of course, Your Highness,' Dave said, bowing to the prince. 'Now, let's get those snacks.'

As Dave hurried on ahead, I hung back to speak with Prince Raju.

'Why is Kapi so protective of you?' I asked.

'I'm the Royal Pigeon and he sees it as his duty to keep me safe.' The prince sighed. 'He knows I long to be free but my duty as the Royal Pigeon must come first and that's why I can never leave the palace.'

Suddenly I understood why the prince was at the wall earlier. 'That's why we saw you at the gate. You wanted to see the outside world, didn't you, Your Highness?'

'It's one of my greatest wishes, Skipper.' The prince sighed again. 'My wings dream of flying beyond the iron bars but alas they never shall.'

Before we could speak further, Dave bounced over. 'Hurry up, you two! There are royal snacks to be eaten.'

'Come with me, my new friends,' Prince Raju laughed, waving us over to the left of the courtyard.

I couldn't wait to tell Granny that little old me was rubbing wings with the actual Royal Pigeon.

The prince led us across the cobbled square and towards the smell of hay and cut grass. A horse, loaded up with a saddle trimmed in gold and velvet, watched us cross the yard, before throwing his head high and shaking his long tousled mane in the breeze. He tipped his head at Prince Raju as we passed.

Beyond the stables was a place that looked a lot like racing pigeon homes. Only larger, grander and far more sparkly.

'Welcome to the Royal Lofts.' Prince Raju beamed.

Dave's beak hung open the whole time as we followed the Royal Pigeon around the birdy palace. We'd heard rumours about the Royal Lofts but never believed them to be true. As squabs, every year on Leftover-Christmas-Chocolates-with-the-Orange-Cream-from-the-Bin Day, my Uncle Constantinos would sit us down and tell us how he once saw the velvet and marble-lined lofts, where the Royal Pigeon family lay in beds of gold and drank diamond water. We always thought this was just a fairy tale that uncles told their squabs because Uncle Constantinos was known for being a massive fibber.

'It's true,' Dave said, astounded. 'The stories of the Royal Lofts are true, Skipper.'

There were beds laden with gold straw and crystal water bottles for every pigeon. Prince Raju led us up a short ladder to a room with his name on a silver plaque above, lined with plush velvet and tiny silk cushions.

'You live here?' Dave asked, his eyes almost popping out of his head in amazement. He ran his wing over the smooth pillows, stroking the soft fabric against his feathers.

The prince flung himself on to a pile of golden straw. 'It's not as glamorous as you think it is.'

He was right. It was MORE glamorous.

He leaned over the side of his bed and pecked at a bowl of colourful seeds. Me and Dave flapped over to join him.

'Do you like *mukhwas*?' he asked.

The bright green and red kernels smelt of peppermint and rose candy and fizzed in my beak.

'I've never tasted seeds like this before,' I said as Dave scoffed down huge beakfuls of the *mukhwas*.

'It is one of my favourite snacks from India,' Prince Raju said. 'My family made sure we had a good supply when we moved here from our palace in Bangalore.'

The roof of the loft shifted and I grabbed Dave's good wing to steady myself. Light poured in as the top opened. Two podgy Human hands reached in and lifted Prince Raju up, reminding me of our Human Lady when she came to visit us in our shed. He cooed as the Human stroked his feathers and rubbed his head.

After placing the prince gently back down, the Human hands reached in again

and fixed a framed painting of Prince Raju
on the wall of the loft by his bed.

'Who is this?' I asked, as the hands
rubbed my head. They smelt of toast
crumbs and clamminess, just like our
Human Lady's hands did.

'That is the Human Princess.'

The roof clicked back on to the loft and I watched as Prince Raju admired the new picture on his wall. He beckoned me over

and we walked along the length of his room, his wing waving at pictures of his relatives in gilded frames.

'That was my great-great-great-grandmother, the original Royal Pigeon. She was a gift from the Indian Royal Humans and was the British Human Queen's favourite,' he said, pointing at the stern-looking pigeon in a necklace of pearls.

'Did you come here from India?' I asked.

'My ancestors did,' the prince replied. 'The British Royal Humans travelled to India many years ago. They fell in love with the people, the tea and the pigeons of course. When my great-great-great-grandmother settled here, the family stayed. My sister Niyanta and I were born in these very lofts.'

'You have an amazing life here,' Dave called out from the other side of the room. '*Mukhwas*, velvet blankets, soft cushions . . . I'd do anything to have a day in your claws.'

'And I would do anything to trade places with you for a day and escape these palace gates,' Prince Raju said. 'I'd love to, just once, hang around a park waiting for picnicking Humans to leave their baskets unattended. What I would give to live like a regular pigeon, foraging for berries and smelling the fresh food growing in the trees.'

That prince may be a prince but he's a bit daft, isn't he? Food doesn't grow on trees.

Of course it does. Where do you think apples, bananas and coconuts come from?

They grow in supermarket aisles and shopping trolleys, obviously.

'We do have a pigeontastic life,' Dave agreed smugly. He puffed out his chest feathers. 'We have our own shed, where we keep our biscuits. At the end of our garden is a Human Lady's house so if we ever run out of snacks we can just fly over and look really sad and she feeds us straight out of her hands.'

'A shed full of biscuits,' the prince said wistfully. 'That sounds divine.'

Dave skipped over to us and stroked Prince Raju's royal robe. 'Can I try this on?'

'Of course, my friend.' Prince Raju pecked at a gold clasp and unhooked the cape. He helped Dave slide it over his slinged wing. 'It suits you.'

Dave had a strange look on his face. The sort of look he had when he was about to suggest a plan. A particularly catbrained scheme that would land us in a mess messier than a pigeon-poo-covered statue. As the pigeons stood side by side, gazing at themselves in a huge mirror, a smile stretched across Dave's beak.

'I have an idea,' he said.

4
The Royal Pecking Order

'Let's swap for a day!' Dave blurted out.

'Swap what?' came a voice from behind us.

We turned to see a pigeon climb up the ladder to join us in Prince Raju's room. Her head was held high and she was wearing a miniature golden tiara, covered in tiny rubies, that balanced on her head. It glittered as she passed across the room, stalking straight towards Dave.

'Well?' she said, raising her head even higher, her voice snooty with disgust as she regarded me for the briefest of seconds.

She looked at Dave. She looked at Prince Raju. She looked back at Dave. Dave looked at her. He looked at me. He looked back at her. She looked at Dave again. She looked at me again. She looked back at Dave again. Dave looked down at his feathery tummy. Then he looked back up at the pigeon.

'What do you want, Niyanta?' Prince Raju said.

'How dare you address me, you common wood pigeon!' Princess Niyanta crowed at her brother. Her grey face turned red with anger. 'Only my brother Prince Raju may address me by my first name.'

She reached over to Dave and yanked him round to face her. 'Raju, get rid of the scruff of a pigeon that looks a lot like you or I will send him to the dungeon.'

'But I'm Dave,' Dave said.

'I'm not in the mood for your ridiculous games.' Niyanta sighed, letting go of my friend. 'How you became the Royal Pigeon, I will never know.'

'I'll go,' the prince muttered, flashing me an apologetic look. He hurried out of the room leaving me, Dave and Princess Niyanta staring at each other.

This was not good and the panicky gurgling in my stomach was about to give us away.

'Who's that?' the princess said, staring

down her beak at me.

'That's Skipper,' Dave said.

'I'm the new valet,' I said hastily, so Dave wouldn't reveal who we really were.

'What happened to Kapi?' Princess Niyanta demanded.

'He . . . errr . . . he . . .' Dave started.

'He's gone on a valet training day,' I blurted.

'Good,' the princess said. 'He could do with the help.'

'I'm the new valet,' I said again, wiping the nervous sweat on my brow. I pointed to Dave. 'And he's the regular old Prince Raju.'

'Yes I am,' Dave said. 'And I do and say regular old prince things like I've always done because I'm the regular old, good old prince.'

The room fell silent.

Silent.

Just long looooong silence.

See? It's still silent.

Dave cleared his throat and stood up straight. 'Come and scratch my itch, valet,' he ordered me.

'What?' I said, wishing we could go back to the silence.

Princess Niyanta groaned. 'Where *do* you find these bozos, Raju?' She came close, our beaks almost touching. 'HE SAID SCRATCH HIS ITCH.'

With the princess's eyes on me, I had no choice but to drag my claws over to Dave. Dave bounced on to Prince Raju's golden bed and lay back, shoving his feet in my face.

I shuddered as my beak made contact with my best friend's foot. Now I'm sure you've all had to scratch a friend's foot before but no one has claws like Dave. NO ONE. Think of the stinkiest cheese in the world, shove a fart in it and cover it in cheesy puffs and that's still not as bad as Dave's feet.

'Up a bit, Skipper,' Dave said, as my beak nuzzled between the pink webs of his claws. 'Left a bit now.'

'I haven't got time to watch this, Raju,' the princess cawed. 'I just came to tell you the Royal Court will be convening later today. Don't be late.' She turned hard on her claws and stamped her way out of the prince's room, her tail feathers fanned out as she clucked and tutted all the way across the loft.

I leaped back from Dave's feet and dunked my head in the prince's water bowl.

'Pah!' I spat, when I'd dried off. 'Can't you wash your feet once in a while, Dave?'

'I could,' Dave said. 'But then I'd lose that lovely wholesome claw smell I've spent years building up.'

It was one of the worst stenches ever to fill my nose holes, and I once fell beak first into a fresh dog poo.

'I'm so sorry,' Prince Raju exclaimed, rushing back into his room. 'My sister is always popping her beak in where it's not needed. She's not too pleased that I was named the Royal Pigeon. She thinks it should've been her.'

Prince Raju walked over to the wall of paintings, gazing upon his ancestors. 'To be quite honest, I would rather it *had* been

her. I long for a life free of responsibilities, free of royal pressures.'

'She thought I was you and you were me, didn't she?' Dave said slowly.

'I guess we really do look alike if my sister can't tell us apart,' Prince Raju said with a smirk.

Prince Raju looked at Dave and looked back at himself in the mirror. 'Dave, about your plan to swap for the day,' he said. He hesitated before he spoke again. 'I think it is the best plan a pigeon has ever suggested in the history of pigeon plans!'

He swung his wing around Dave's shoulder and they grinned at each other in the mirror.

'Hand me that sling, old chap,' Prince Raju said, trying to imitate Dave's voice. 'And let's swap lives.'

'Hang on,' I cried. 'You can't just pretend to be each other.'

Prince Raju ignored me and slipped on Dave's sling and Medal of the Brave. He tugged the golden cuff off his ankle before squeezing it on to Dave's leg.

'How do I look?' Prince Raju said,

as Dave nodded approvingly. 'I need to fit in perfectly in the outside world.'

'I'm not sure about this,' I said, louder this time. Dave knew nothing about being a prince and the prince knew nothing about being a Dave. My claws curled in panic at the thought of Dave being found out, sending the two of us on a one-way ticket back to the dungeon. My head bobbed from one pigeon to the other. I couldn't tell who was who in the exchange of robes and sling and flying feathers. 'Dave, you don't know the first thing about being a Royal Pigeon.'

'Don't worry, Skipper,' Dave said. At least I think it was Dave. 'How hard can it be?'

The prince piped up. 'It's just for a day

and then we'll swap back.'

'Just a day?' I said, unsure.

'Of course,' Prince Raju said. Though it might have been Dave. 'Stop worrying, Skipper.'

'What is going on here?' a voice boomed across Prince Raju's room.

Kapi stood by the entrance to the room with his wings on his waist and his nose holes fuming.

'Kapi!' Prince Raju said, delighted. 'You're just in time.'

'Why is that imposter in here and why is he wearing your robes?' Kapi demanded.

There was no fooling Kapi, who clearly

64

knew the prince better than Princess Niyanta did.

Prince Raju pulled Kapi close and whispered Dave's plan to him.

'No, Sire,' Kapi said, shaking his head hard. 'No, no, no, no, no, no, no. I simply forbid it.'

'Kapi,' Prince Raju said, standing tall. 'Am I the Royal Pigeon?'

'Yes, Sire.'

'And do I not make the decisions around here?' Prince Raju continued.

'But, Sire! This is far too dangerous.'

'Kapi?' Prince Raju said, raising his eyebrows at his valet.

'Yes, Sire,' Kapi said, his voice small. 'You make the decisions.'

'This will be so good for me,' the prince said, slapping Kapi on the back. 'You'll see.'

'And what am I supposed to do, Sire?' Kapi challenged.

'You'll swap places with Skipper of course,' Dave said.

'We don't look anything alike,' I said, waving my wing from me to Kapi and back to me again.

'It's fine, Skipper,' Dave said. 'The princess thinks you are the prince's new valet. No one will question it.'

'Dave's right,' Prince Raju said. 'You mustn't worry.'

But I was worried. 'What if we get found out?'

'Stay out of Niyanta's way, my

friends, and you'll be fine,' Prince Raju said, grabbing Kapi before he could object and dashing off down the ladder. 'We've got a shed full of biscuits to discover.'

'Wait!' I called out.

But it was too late.

Dave (who was now Prince Raju) and I watched as Prince Raju (who was now Dave) and Kapi barrelled out of the lofts and raced for the gate beyond.

And then they were gone.

And Dave was the Royal Pigeon.

Here is my list of royal demands, Skipper.
Royal biscuits at 7 am
Royal biscuits at 7:01 am
Royal biscuits at 7:02 am
Royal biscuits at 7:03 am
Royal biscuits at 7:04 am
Royal biscuits at 7:05 am
Royal biscuits at 7:06 am
Royal biscuits at 7:07 am
Royal biscuits at 7:08 am
Royal biscuits at 7:09 am
Royal biscuits at 7:10 am
Royal biscuits at 7:11 am
Royal biscuits at 7:12 am
You'd better read on. Dave might be here a while.

5

Dave Gets the Royal Tweetment

'What are you going to do, Dave?' I panicked. 'You don't know anything about being the Royal Pigeon.'

'How hard can it be?' Dave said, admiring his new robes in the mirror. 'Let's get ourselves some royal snacks,' he continued calmly. 'And don't worry, Skipper, you can still call me Dave. I wouldn't want you to feel the pressure to call me "Your

Highness" or "Your Majesty".'

'Dave! You aren't the real Royal Pigeon,' I said. 'No one is going to call you "Your Highness".'

'Your Highness, the Royal Humans have delivered the loft catering,' came a stiff voice from the foot of the small ladder. 'Will you be taking your elevenses now?'

'Yes,' Dave said, in his most royal of voices. 'Your Highness will be taking elevenses now and will be looking forward to some royal snacks.'

The pigeon at the ladder popped his head up. 'And your friend, Your Highness?' he asked, looking at me.

'This is Skipper, my new valet, and he will be joining me,' Dave said. 'Because

I am Your Highness and I say so.'

'Very well,' the pigeon said.

Dave and me trailed down the ladder behind the slim pigeon.

'Hold the bottom of my robe, will you, Skipper?' Dave cawed.

I gritted my beak and picked the robe off Dave's bottom as we carried on through the lofts. In the last twenty minutes, I'd spent more time than any pigeon should ever have to up close to Dave's feet and bottom. If he made me do one more ridiculous thing, I would walk straight over to the dungeon and lock myself in to save my poor nose holes.

'What's your name?' I asked the slim pigeon, who was watching me and Dave out of the side of his eye.

'I am His Highness's butler, Sir,' the pigeon said. 'They call me Butler.'

He took us into a room where a golden ledge was lined with barley, corn and millet. On the opposite side there was minced carrot and broccoli and tiny shreds of lettuce.

'What is this?' Dave asked, confused by the healthy buffet.

'Elevenses, Your Highness,' Butler said. 'Your buffet, as always, was selected by the Royal Humans.' He hopped back to let us through. 'Will that be all, Your Highness?'

Dave wasn't listening. He hunted along the shelves of food, his head bobbing up and down. I nodded at Butler, who left quickly.

'Where are the biscuits?' Dave whispered to me.

I shrugged and nibbled at the barley. It was surprisingly delicious despite looking like something a rabbit would poo. 'You should try this, Dave,' I said, scooping up a beakful of carrot and millet. 'It's really good.'

Dave poked his beak in the corn.

'I'm only going to eat this because it would be rude not to, but Your Highness is very disappointed by the lack of biscuits and chocolate cake.'

Dave gobbled up as much as he could before hiccupping and lying back in a heap in the middle of the room.

'You know, Skipper, this Royal Pigeon stuff is easy,' he said, staring at the ornate ceiling of the loft. Paintings of pigeons from yesteryear filled the roof space, surrounding a huge crystal chandelier which dangled, dripping with sparkles, from the centre of the ceiling.

'Nothing could ruin this moment now—'

'How have you got time to lie around with all your Royal Pigeon duties?'

It was Princess Niyanta.

Oh no.

Dave struggled to get to his feet as the princess sauntered in. He rolled around on the floor like a beetle on its back.

'Hwho is THAT?' came a high-pitched cry.

Double oh no.

A dainty female pigeon stepped out from behind the princess. She screwed her beak up at me.

'That's the new valet,' Princess Niyanta said.

'I'm   Palomi,'

the pigeon trilled at me. 'I'm Princess Niyanta's lady's maid. How d'you do?'

She had a way of adding extra letters to words that made it sound like she was telling me off.

Princess Niyanta pecked at the millet before stopping so Palomi could brush away the seeds from her beak.

'Raju, we need to go over your timetable for the day,' the princess announced.

Dave didn't move.

'Raju?' Princess Niyanta tried again. 'Your timetable?'

Dave still didn't move.

I shot Dave a look. He'd forgotten he was wearing the Royal Pigeon's robes and was supposed to be Prince Raju. Before he ignored the princess any longer, I blurted out 'Your Highness' at him.

'I knew you'd come round, Skipper,' Dave said, oblivious to the suspicious looks on Palomi and Princess Niyanta's faces.

'I haven't got all day, Raju,' the princess said. Dave plonked himself down and the princess began.

'This morning you have a photo shoot. It's the official Royal Pigeon portrait so don't stuff it up,' she said.

'That sounds easy enough,' Dave said.

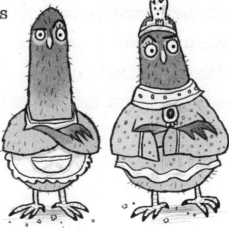

'After that, you are opening the new bird bath in the yard and meeting fans,' Princess Niyanta continued.

'Even easier,' Dave said, smirking. 'Being the Royal Pigeon is simple, simpler than taking a jammy biscuit from Skipper when he's sleeping.'

'Hey!' I said. 'I knew I was one short.'

'Then,' the princess continued, 'you have a luncheon with the Royal Pigeon of Belgium, followed by playtime with the Human Princess and her friends, then flight training before your meeting with the Royal Pigeon of Monaco, then a photo shoot with the Royal Pigeon of Brunei, before the evening audience with the Royal Court—'

'Hold on, hold on,' Dave said, sticking up his good wing. 'That's a lot for one day. Can't we spread all these things over today and tomorrow or the next year?'

'Then what would happen to all the duties you have *timetabled* for tomorrow and the next year?' the princess scoffed. 'You have to take the position of Royal Pigeon seriously, Raju. It's a privilege to serve the lofts.'

'Your Highness, you are needed for the royal photo shoot,' Butler said, rushing into the buffet room and coaxing Dave out.

'Shall I come with you?' I called after Dave.

'No need,' Butler called back. 'Enjoy your snacks and then you may retire to Prince

Raju's chambers.'

My friend was whisked off before I could say millet rhymes with skillet. I didn't want to spend any more time with the princess and her maid so I gulped down a beakful of corn and left for Prince Raju's room. As the door swung behind me, I overheard Palomi muttering angrily to Princess Niyanta.

'Hwe have to get rid of him,' Palomi said.

'Don't be silly,' the princess said. 'He's my brother.'

'He may be hyour brother,' Palomi replied. 'But hyou deserve to be Royal Pigeon.'

'I suppose.'

'If Prince Raju has a bad day today and

puts a few beaks out of jhoint, the Royal Court hwill have no choice but to name hyou Royal Pigeon. Corvus and I hwill see to it.' Palomi sniggered. 'Hyou'll have to excuse me, Hyour Highness, as I set my plan in mhotion. I *might* have a bit of a surprise already hwaiting for your brother at the photo shoot.'

The two birds cackled with laughter over their plans to ruin Prince Raju.

My friend was in big trouble.

6

Prince Raju Is Free as a Bird

I had to do something. I had to warn Dave.

I rushed back through the buffet room, skidding past the princess, who was now alone and heading in the direction that Dave and Butler had gone. Dave was nowhere to be found. I hurried through the lofts, racing around every gilded corner. There was pigeon after pigeon but not a single one in a purple royal robe. My heart was going at a million miles an hour, like

a pigeon on a hamster wheel. The longer I spent searching for Dave, the more time Palomi had for her evil plans.

'AYEEEEEEE!'

I knew that ayeeeeee. That was Dave's cry when he'd got his bottom stuck in something.

'AYEEEEEEE!'

Flying out of the lofts, I followed the shriek to the courtyard. There I saw a small crowd of Humans, one with a camera who was shouting and screaming at the other Humans.

'AH AH AH AH AYE EEEEEEEEEEEEEEE EEEEEEEEEEEEEEE!' I soared high to get a better view. My friend was on a wooden

stage in the centre of the courtyard. And he was dancing.

I dived down and landed on the stone floor by the stage. Dave was dancing but not in his usual Dave-dancing way. He was wiggling his bottom and shuffling it along the stage.

'I cannot work with this pigeon,' the Camera Human bellowed. 'He is impossible. He refuses to stand still.'

'Dave,' I hissed. 'You need to be still. You are messing up the whole shoot.'

'I can't,' Dave sobbed. 'There's something wrong with my bum-bum.'

He waved his tail in my face and I could see now why he had been dancing in such a strange way. He hadn't been dancing at all. His bottom was red and raw, and it looked like he'd sat in a plate of jam.

But he hadn't sat in jam.

As Dave shook his bottom again, I saw something. There, on the stage, right under Dave's tail, was a nest.

'What is going on—' I started.

A shadow near the back of the stage caught my eye. As I peered round I saw Palomi. She was staring at the nest.

And she was gloating.

I followed her gaze. The knotted twigs in the nest appeared to be crawling. Crawling with teeny, tiny, bitey insects.

Pigeon mites!

'You need to get off the stage,' I screeched at my friend. 'It's covered in pigeon mites.'

Dave threw himself off the platform and landed his bottom on the cool cobblestones.

'Your Highness, are you OK?' Butler cried, hurtling over to Dave.

'Pigeon mites,' Dave whimpered. 'I have pigeon mites.'

'Let's get you in a bath,' Butler said, helping Dave to his feet and leading him to the lofts. 'The photo shoot is over anyway because the Humans are unhappy.'

Palomi had sabotaged my friend.

And now Dave was hurt.

I had to find Prince Raju. He'd know what to do.

I squeezed back through the hole in the gate and out to the street. Pigeons littered the pavements in enormous crowds, munching snacks and twittering to each other.

Landing on the wall, I looked over the hordes of birds. I couldn't see Prince Raju anywhere. Had he already left for the shed?

Jumping down, I joined the grey feathery mass of pigeons. I recognised Mickey among them.

'Have you seen a pigeon who looks like

Dave?' I asked him.

'You mean Dave?' Mickey said. He offered me some sticky popcorn that he'd already pecked.

I shook my head no at the popcorn. My stomach was churning with worry and I had no appetite for a sweet treat, even if it was scrumptious fizzy orange flavour.

'No. Well, yes. I mean Dave but just Dave for today.'

'Sorry,' Mickey said. 'I've seen Dave but not Dave-for-Today.'

'That's who I mean,' I said, remembering no one else knew Prince Raju was pretending to be Dave. 'You've seen Dave?'

'Yes.'

'Where is he?'

'I think he went back to the shed,' Mickey said. 'He was acting very strangely. He didn't even give his old man a hug. And he kept asking the quickest way to the shed.'

'Did you tell him?'

'Of course, but I reminded him he couldn't fly because of his broken wing and then the other pigeon with him told me he would have me thrown in the dungeon for saying such things.'

'Sorry about that, Mickey,' I said. 'Dave's not quite himself today.'

I took off towards the shed, flying over the streets which now were not only packed with pigeons but also buses and cars and Humans with heavy shopping bags.

It didn't take me long to get home, and it was a lot quicker than having to get the train with Dave. I found a confused-looking Mean Cat sniffing at the shed door. She could probably smell Prince Raju was not

Dave. And that Kapi wasn't me. I dived towards the open window so she couldn't take a swipe at me and landed on two heaps of feathers snoring among the old paint cans.

'Prince Raju?' I said, shaking him awake.

'Skipper,' he said. 'There's an awful yowling beastie out there. Get rid of it will you, my good man. Send it to the dungeon if you have to.'

'That's Mean Cat,' I said. 'And there's no

getting rid of her. Believe me, we've tried.'

The prince got to his feet and stretched out his wings. His shoulders were relaxed and his face was no longer screwed up. He looked happy. Happy and free.

'Oh, Skipper, this is magnificent!' he said, dancing from paint can lid to paint can lid. 'I feel wonderful. Your life on this side of the royal gate is unrestricted and full of joy. I ate a biscuit for the first time and I've never eaten anything so delicious.'

I looked at the crumpled packet thrown on the floor. They were the jammy ones. My favourites. 'You've eaten *all* our biscuits.'

'You don't mind, do you?' Prince Raju said. 'You're welcome to eat any palace food you want.'

HE THINKS MILLET IS AS GOOD AS BISCUITS?

It was good millet.

It was, BUT STILL!

I took a breath. I was here for Dave, not to discuss the prince eating my favourite biscuits.

'You need to come back to the lofts,' I said.

'But we agreed to swap for the day,' Kapi

said, who was relaxing in the soft nest of papers stacked by my trusty typewriter. He'd certainly taken to shed life despite his objections at the Royal Lofts. 'In fact, I'm thinking of asking Prince Raju to make this change more permanent.'

This was getting worse quickly.

'Yoo hoo!' came the chirp of our next-door neighbour, Tinkles.

This was getting worse VERY quickly. Tinkles always had a way of showing up right at the time when I could do without a nosy canary poking her beak in.

The pristine yellow ball of feathers landed at the window and tapped on the

glass with her tiny beak.

'Who is *this* delightful sight?' Prince
Raju said, headbutting the window open to
let Tinkles squeeze through.

I'm not sure I'd ever describe Tinkles as
'delightful'.

'What a strange thing to say, Dave!' Tinkles exclaimed at the prince. 'Although I suppose you might not recognise me with my brand-new, cooling, heat-activated sparkle headband.'

'That's a smashing headband,' Prince Raju said, bowing to the yellow fuzz ball. 'Would you care to dance?'

Dave would *never* dance with Tinkles. If Prince Raju wasn't careful he would blow his cover.

'Oh my.' Tinkles giggled. 'I do like this new version of you, Dave.'

The flap of Tinkles's tiny wings whipped up a small wind and raised Dave's sling off the prince's tummy. His wing! If Tinkles got any closer, she would see his unbroken wing and know for sure he wasn't Dave. And then there would be questions, so many questions, and a canary heading straight to the palace to have me and Dave thrown in the dungeon.

'Wait!' I cried. 'You promised me a dance first, Dave.'

I squished my body between Tinkles and the prince and bopped the canary away with my bottom.

'Kapi, you dance with Tinkles,' Prince Raju said, twirling me around on the shelf and flipping me over his back.

The prince and Kapi tapped out a beat and Tinkles chirruped along. For the first time since I'd arrived at the shed, I felt lighter and happier as Prince Raju told me

stories of his first biscuit and we danced wing in wing.

'Dance-off,' Kapi cried.

Prince Raju spun me towards Kapi, who spun Tinkles towards Prince Raju. Kapi caught my wing and pulled me into a circle with the others. Prince Raju jumped into the middle, kicking up his claws as we flapped our wings to the beat.

'Princess Niyanta and her lady's maid are planning to make things difficult for Dave,' I whispered to Kapi, telling him all about the pigeon mites at the royal photo shoot.

'Ah yes, Palomi. She's a bit of a pain, isn't she?'

Tinkles and the prince continued their

dance battle as Kapi and I stepped away.

Kapi picked at a splinter of wood in the nearby shelf. He pulled it free and wiped at the crumbs and biscuit jam stuck to his beak. 'Palomi has a habit of getting in the princess's head with her shifty plans.'

'Will you come back and help Dave?' I asked.

'The trouble is, old chum, it is very hard to care when you feel as free as a bird.'

'But Dave doesn't know anything about being the Royal Pigeon,' I said. 'Prince Raju *needs* to come back and help him.'

'He doesn't,' Kapi said. 'He doesn't have

any responsibilities now. He is Dave after all.' He plopped back into his paper nest. 'Here's the thing, Skipper. If you ask His Highness to return, don't you think you'll be putting the prince in danger if, like you said, Palomi and the princess are hatching evil plans?' He turned over and fluffed up the paper padding. 'Now be a good fellow and enough with the questions. I think I'll have a nap.'

I watched Prince Raju twirl and skip with Tinkles. Kapi was right. It was up to me to help both my friends. And I had to get back to the Royal Lofts fast, before Palomi got her claws on Dave.

7

A Coup in the Coop

'This is a coup!'

I arrived back at the palace just in time to see Princess Niyanta and Palomi gather a crowd of pigeon troops and march them towards the Royal Lofts. Palomi yelled out the princess's name and the mob chanted it back.

I squeezed my way through the flock of feathery bodies towards the ladder to the prince's room.

'No! This is a coo,' Dave crowed back at

the crowd. 'COOOOO!'

'A coup, you fool,' Palomi shrieked.
'C-O-U-P!'

The chant of 'Princess Niyanta,
Princess Niyanta' grew squawkier and
squawkier from the troops.

'Skipper!' Dave shrieked as I scampered up towards him. He hurled his body at mine and hugged me hard.

'What happened?' I asked, picking us both off the floor.

'It's been awful, Skipper,' Dave said. 'I thought I'd be dining on royal biscuits and splashing my feet in the diamond water of the royal bird bath but instead I've been bitten by pigeon mites, forgotten the names of all the Royal Pigeons and where they come from, and now the princess is going to throw me in the dungeon because of my coo.'

'It's a coup, Dave. She's planning to overthrow you,' I said, panicked.

'I can't go back to the dungeon, Skipper,' Dave wailed. 'I can't.' He dragged me behind the mirror. 'Let's take cover here so no one finds us. Can you believe the Royal Court is demanding I meet with them? I'm the Royal Pigeon. I should demand to meet with them!'

'Dave!' I said, shaking my friend by the shoulders. 'You are not the Royal Pigeon!'

Don't say it. Don't say 'I told you so'.
I won't.
I see you thinking it.
I am thinking it.
Stop it.
I can't stop it! You put it in my head now!
And now I have taken it out.
I'm still thinking it.
Skipper!

Dave held up his good wing. 'Look at these worn and tired wings. I've been at photo shoots. I've had to sign letters to royal fans. I've had to open a new bird bath in town and make a speech and I haven't had a single biscuit for my troubles.'

He pulled me close. 'And then I came back to the lofts to find everyone was annoyed with me because I was supposed to have a luncheon with the Royal Pigeon of Belgium then meet with the Royal Pigeon of Monaco and then have a photo shoot with the Royal Pigeon of Brunei. Only I had lunch with the Monaco pigeon and told the Belgium pigeon to meet with the Brunei pigeon whilst I had a nap because I was definitely not going to another photo shoot after this morning.' Dave scratched his head. 'Or was it the Belgium pigeon that met with the Monaco pigeon?'

'This isn't your fault, Dave,' I explained. 'Palomi wants everyone against you so Princess Niyanta can be the Royal Pigeon.'

'She's so mean.'

'Dave,' I said gently. 'What are you going to do?'

'Let's go back to our wonderful shed! We'll find Prince Raju and swap again.'

I looked down at the floor.

'What's wrong, Skipper?'

My throat felt like dry oat flakes. I gulped and tried to find the words.

'It's Prince Raju,' I said. 'We can't bring him back to this.'

'Why not?'

'I just saw him,' I continued. 'I knew Palomi was plotting with the princess so I went to get help.'

'Where was he?'

'He was in our shed, eating our biscuits.'

'WHAT?!'

'He's so happy and free, Dave.'

'HE WAS EATING OUR BISCUITS?!'

'Dave!' I squawked. 'You are missing the important bit.'

'If you say biscuits, I'm going to focus on that, Skipper.'

'If we bring him back now, we might put him in danger,' I said. 'He's our friend.'

Dave screwed up his beak. 'But I want biscuits.'

'And we'll have all the biscuits we want if we help out the prince,' I said. I could see Dave struggling to think beyond shortbread and cookies. 'Think of all the biscuits you'll have when everyone finds out you're a hero.'

'Hero biscuits *are* especially yummy.' Dave looked at the velvet robe on his shoulders. 'You're right, Skipper. We must protect the Royal Pigeon. And then eat the hero biscuits.'

Before I could say any more, the high-pitched shriek of Palomi pierced my ear holes.

'GET OUT FROM BEHIND THAT MIRROR, PRINCE RAJU,' she screeched. 'SHOW YOURSELF, YOU COWHWARD.'

'I'm not Prince Raju, I'm Dave,' Dave pleaded, shuffling out of his hiding place.

'You are out of time, Raju,' the princess said, ignoring what my friend had said. 'By order of the pigeons of the Royal Lofts, you are being exiled.'

'Exiled where?' Dave asked.

'Outside to the courtyard for the moment, whilst the Royal Court convenes and decides what to do with you.' The princess turned up her beak at me. 'And you're banished too.'

Corvus grabbed Dave by his robe, kicked me into step and pigeon-marched us to the yard. The crowd of loft pigeons hissed and jeered, turning their backs on Dave one at a time, squawking, 'Off with his beak,' as he stumbled past.

'Stay here whilst the Royal Court assembles,' Corvus crowed at Dave, pushing us both to the ground outside.

Dave clung on to me as Corvus returned to the lofts for his next command from the princess.

'What are we going to do, Dave?' I asked, helping my friend to his feet.

'There is only one thing we can do,' he said, dusting himself off. 'Since I replaced Prince Raju, we need to find a pigeon who looks exactly the same as me to replace me and *they* can deal with Princess Niyanta and the Royal Court.'

8
Looking for a Pigeon Who Fits the Bill

Dave cooed out a call through the hole in the gate, inviting pigeons to audition to become the prince. Within moments birds flocked to the gate. My friend perched on the wall as pigeons squeezed through the gap one after another and presented themselves.

'Name?' he squawked to the first one.

'Sue Wilsher.'

'And what makes you think you could replace me?'

'Ah,' Sue Wilsher the pigeon said. 'Is that what this queue is for?'

'Yes,' I said. 'We're auditioning for someone to stand in for the Royal Pigeon.'

'Oh,' she said. 'I thought this was a school trip.'

'Next?' Dave screeched, rolling his eyes at me.

One by one pigeons auditioned to play the role of Dave playing the role of Prince Raju. Dave's plan wasn't great but it distracted him and gave me time to come up with a better one.

'I can sing,' the next bird said.

'That's not necessary,' I said.

'I'd like to hear,' Dave said.
'I have a wonderful singing
voice.'

Who would like to hear
me sing now, Skipper?

No one. No one wants to
hear you sing. We're at a very
tense part of the story.

Spoilsport.

As I looked down the long queue of
pigeons, my heart felt like it had dropped

right through my gut and out of my poop hole. This was hopeless. The pigeons lined up to see Dave were too tall, too small, too feathery or not feathery enough. There were ones who could warble, ones who couldn't, ones who could play the piano, and ones who were looking for their big break into the pigeon showbiz world. And some weren't even pigeons at all. I was pretty sure, near the end of the queue, there was a small badger that had lost its way, and a nibbled oatmeal cookie.

'Very nice,' Dave said, nodding at the singing pigeon. 'But I'm afraid on this occasion you haven't made it to the next round.'

'Thank you for the opportunity, Your Highness,' the pigeon said, disappointed.

'Next?'

I stepped away from the auditions and soared up into the sky. Between the clouds, I spied the lopsided kitty weathervane on our Human Lady's house. I had to return to the shed. It was the only way I could make sure both Dave and Prince Raju were free but the Royal Lofts were protected.

I found Prince Raju still snoozing in the shed when I arrived. He'd shaken off Dave's sling and turned it into a pillow for his bottom. There was a half-eaten chocolate brioche by his feet that he hadn't managed to finish. He was as terrible at being Dave as Dave was at being Prince Raju.

'You're back again?' Kapi said, waking in his paper den.

'Yes, and I don't care what you say, Prince Raju is going back to the palace and swapping with Dave.'

'No, he's not,' he said, looking me straight in the eye.

'Yes, he is.'

'No, he's not.'

'Yes, he is.'

'No, he's not.'

This went on for a while. A whole chapter in fact.

9
Toucan Play at that Game

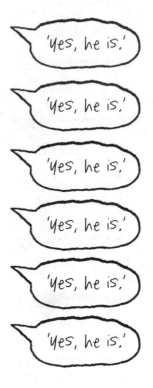

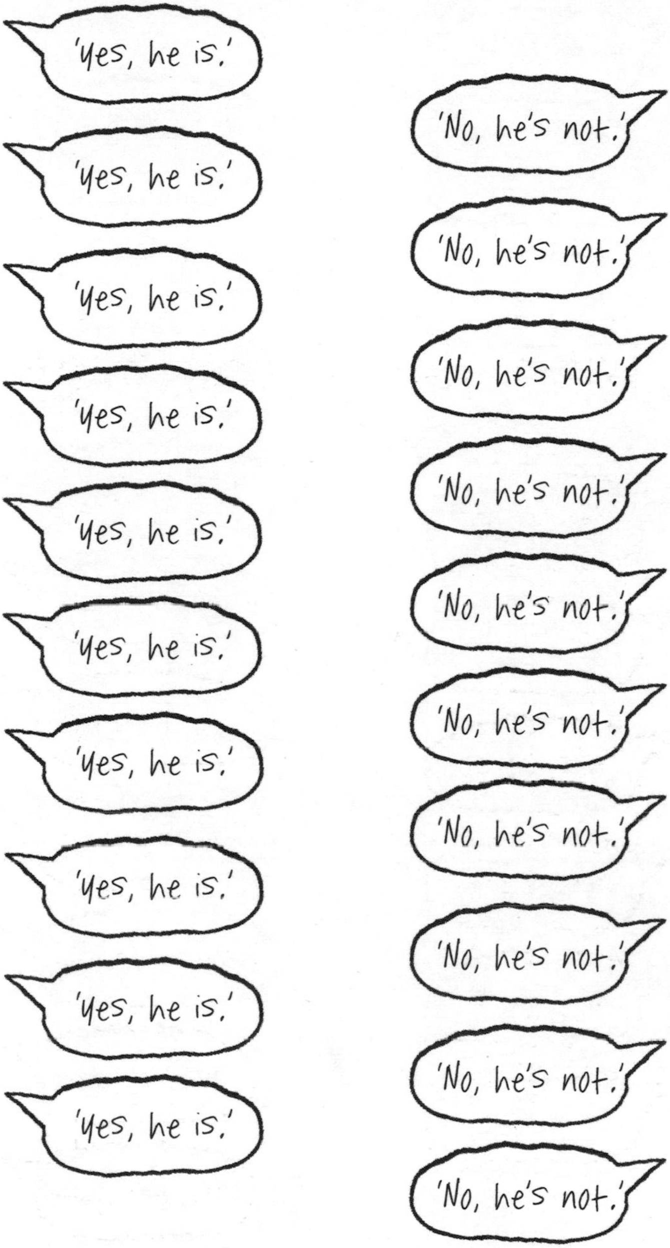

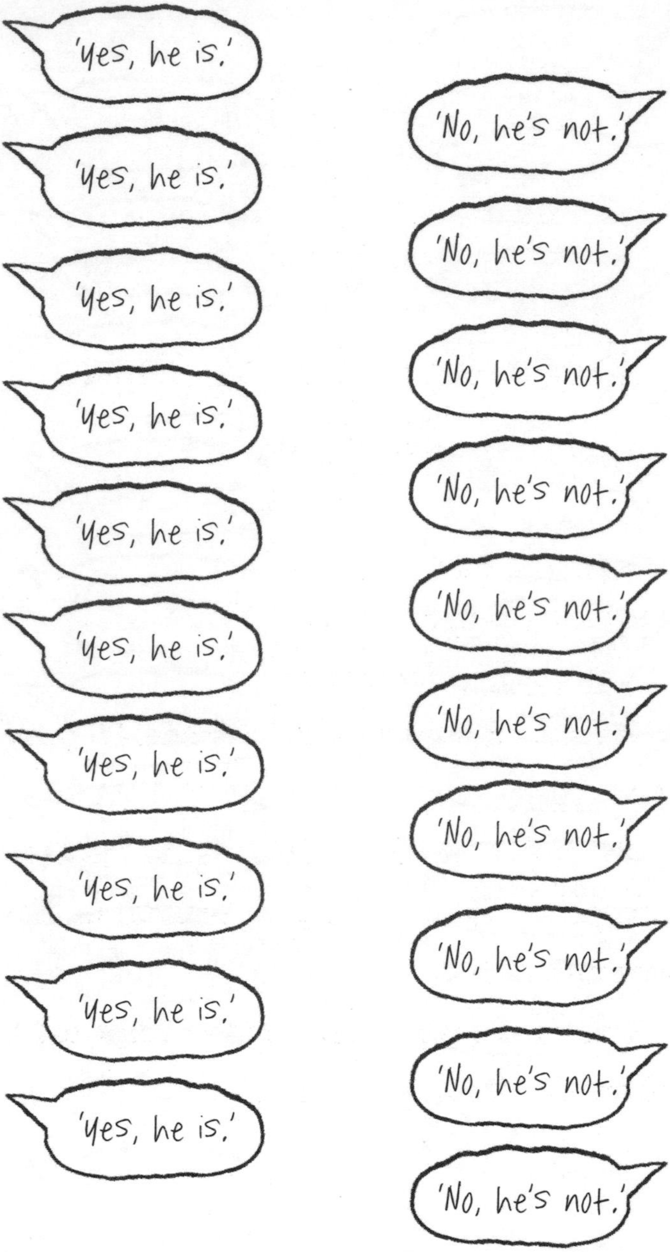

10
Prince Raju Comes Home to Roost

'This is tiring,' Kapi said.

'Let's stop,' I agreed.

We sat side by side on the shelf by my typewriter.

'Dave is holding auditions to replace himself,' I said. 'Being a prince is not for him.'

'That's a pigeontastic idea,' Kapi said. 'Then we can all be free.'

'It's a terrible idea,' I said. 'Because Prince Raju is the Royal Pigeon and no one else can do the job he does. Not Dave. Not Princess Niyanta and not a pigeon who wants to pretend to be Dave who is pretending to be Prince Raju.'

Kapi ran his feathers over the keys of my typewriter. I could see him struggling with his duty to return home, whilst longing to hang on to his new-found freedom. 'I suppose I have become a bit bored without my regular routine.' He nodded towards the prince. 'You can wake him up.'

'Princess Niyanta is staging a coup,' I said, as the prince stretched from his slumber.

'What?' Prince Raju said. He sat up

straight. His grey face turned red as he started to shake with anger. 'How dare she?'

'I did tell Kapi earlier—' I started.

'I didn't want to upset you, Sire,' Kapi interrupted.

'Kapi! You have to stop trying to protect me,' the prince squawked. 'Is what Skipper says true?'

'Yes, Sire,' Kapi said, hanging his head.

'Please return to your position as the Royal Pigeon,' I pleaded.

'Of course! I am the Royal Pigeon, after all,' the prince said. 'And I must protect my friend Dave.'

'I have a plan that might still secure your freedom,' I said. 'You just have to come

back to the Royal Lofts and I'll explain everything.'

We soared through the skies and I could see now why Prince Raju was the Royal Pigeon. He glided through the clouds with the speed and grace of a trained high-velocity racing pigeon. Dave's sling ballooned out behind him like a parachute as Prince Raju looped the loop through the clouds, over Kapi and under the trees.

By the time we arrived, the audition

queue had disappeared and there were just three remaining on the wall.

'Skipper! You are just in time,' Dave said, as the prince and I landed. 'These are the final three.'

'The final three pigeons who are trying out for the part of you as me?' Prince Raju said, raising a sceptical eyebrow at the remaining auditionees. 'Isn't that last one a badger?'

'You're right,' Dave said. 'What a pigeony-looking badger!'

The two birds and the badger stood tall as Dave and Prince Raju inspected them closely.

'None of them are as handsome as we are,' Dave said.

'You are quite right,' Prince Raju said.

They turned to the birds and the badger. 'I'm afraid you won't be going any further in this contest,' Prince Raju said. 'But you should be so proud of yourselves for making it this far.'

The animals scampered away, leaving just me, Dave and Prince Raju in the courtyard.

'Are you back?' Dave asked the prince.

'It depends,' the prince replied. 'Skipper says he has a plan.'

'Well, I'm not going to be the Royal Pigeon a moment longer,' Dave said crossly. 'I have a sore bottom and your sister is very angry with me for not being you, even though she still thinks I am you.' Dave threw up his good wing and shook his head in frustration.

'What now?' Prince Raju said, turning to me. 'Neither of us wants to be prince and both of us want to be free.'

'Did you not miss being the Royal Pigeon

just a little bit?'

'A little,' the prince admitted. His eyes narrowed. 'But I'm furious that my sister is trying to steal my title.'

'This is what we are going to do—' I started.

Butler came rushing into the courtyard and cut me off.

'Your Highness,' he said, out of breath. 'It's time for the Royal Court.'

'Quick! Swap back,' Kapi hissed at Dave and the prince. 'I'll distract Butler.'

He ran at Butler and bowled him off his feet as Dave and Prince Raju traded royal robes and golden cuff for Dave's sling and medal.

'What was that for?' Butler said, as he

and Kapi got to their feet and straightened up their feathers.

'Sorry, Butler,' Kapi said. 'I thought I saw a cat.'

Butler shot us a confused look but cast an eye over the courtyard for any monstrous felines.

'Your Highness, shall we go?' he said, once he was sure it was safe.

'Yes, Butler. Let's face the Royal Court.'

As Kapi and Prince Raju shuffled past me, I turned to the pigeon in the sling.

'Is that you, Dave?' I asked.

'Of course, Skipper,' he said. 'Pigeon's Promise. Cross my heart, hope to die, stick a peanut in my eye.'

11

It's a Penguin—win Situation

The Royal Court was held in the grandest of the Royal Loft spaces: the buffet room. A huge crate, with the letters 'CHAMPAGNE' stamped on the side, now stood in the middle of the room. Eight pigeons sat in the crate in a circle around a throne of gold straw and hay. Princess Niyanta perched next to the throne, scowling at us.

'All stand for the Royal Pigeon,' Butler cried, and everyone rose as Prince Raju joined the circle.

'You may sit,' the prince declared.

One of the older pigeons looked at Dave. She looked at Prince Raju. She looked back at Dave. Dave looked at the pigeon. He looked at me. He looked back at the pigeon. The pigeon looked at Dave again. She looked at me again. She looked back at Dave again. Dave looked down at his feathery tummy. Then he looked back up at the pigeon.

'Who are they?' the pigeon asked, nodding at Dave and me.

'I'm Skipper,' I said. 'And this is Dave.'

'And what do you want?' she asked.

'They are here as my friends,' Prince Raju said.

Prince Raju glided towards the middle of

the circle and took his place on the golden throne whilst his sister glared at him.

'There is unrest in the Royal Lofts,' the oldest of the pigeons said. She wore a string of pearls around her neck and reminded me of the picture of Prince Raju's great-great-great-grandmother that hung in his room.

'I know,' Prince Raju said, lowering his head. 'And I am as unhappy about that as you are.'

'I think it's time for a new Royal Pigeon,' Princess Niyanta said. 'Today, we almost had an international disaster when Prince Raju had lunch with His Royal Highness of Monaco and ate *both* of their lunches.'

Dave shrugged and gave me his best

'I thought I was supposed to eat two lunches' face.

The princess threw back her head and her pearly turquoise feathers shimmered in the crystal light. 'All in favour of appointing a new Royal Pigeon, raise your wing now.'

Slowly, wings went up, one by one.

I leaped up, dragging Dave with me. 'Before you finish voting, I have an idea,' I said.

We hopped forward and bowed to the circle of pigeons. I mouthed the words 'Trust me' to Prince Raju, who lowered his head at me to continue.

'How dare you address the court without being asked?' Palomi screeched, jumping

out from behind the princess and shooting me an evil glare.

'I've invited Skipper to speak,' Prince Raju said. Palomi's beak hung open in shock.

I took a breath before I spoke. 'Prince Raju needs to be allowed the freedom to leave the Royal Lofts,' I said.

There was a gasp from the circle as all the pigeons looked at me wide-eyed.

'But no Royal Pigeon has ever left the Royal Lofts,' Princess Niyanta said.

'Wouldn't the Royal Pigeon be a better pigeon if he could get out of the palace, talk to the pigeons beyond the gate and find out how they live?' I looked at Dave, who nodded me on. 'The prince has to make very important decisions about pigeons all the time. Wouldn't it make sense that he goes out into the world and experiences it? The more he experiences and understands different pigeons, the better and fairer his decisions will be. We wouldn't want a Royal Pigeon who was out of touch with the ordinary pigeons, would we?'

Some of the pigeons started to mutter in agreement. Princess Niyanta's nose holes flared as she watched the older pigeons.

'That sounds like a sensible suggestion,' the oldest pigeon said. 'I've always fancied a trip to the seaside myself.'

'What about the royal duties?' Princess Niyanta scoffed. 'Are the lofts abandoned every time the Royal Pigeon wants a holiday?'

'I suggest someone else takes over when Prince Raju is out,' I replied.

'Like who?' the princess demanded.

'Like you, dear sister,' Prince Raju suggested. I grinned: the prince had worked out the final piece of my plan.

'Me?' Princess Niyanta said. Her beak fell open.

'If we share being the Royal Pigeon, will you stop battling with me?' Prince Raju asked his sister.

Her eyes narrowed. 'In exchange for what?'

Prince Raju held out his wing and whispered behind it to his sister, 'Perhaps you could have a word with Palomi about not being quite so mean?'

'Fine,' Princess Niyanta said, clapping her wing against his outstretched one.

'We'll make a fine team if we are on the same side,' the prince said. He turned to the court. 'All in favour, raise a wing.'

Wings shot up high in the air.

'I have one final suggestion,' the prince said. He reached under his feathers, ruffling between the grey and turquoise, before pulling out a biscuit. A jammy biscuit. 'Perhaps we could add biscuits to the royal menu?' The prince winked at Dave. 'What do you think, Dave?'

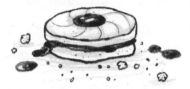

'I think that is a pigeontastic suggestion,' Dave said, launching towards the biscuit.

As the Royal Court finished discussing their Royal Pigeon business, and with Dave back to being Dave and Prince Raju back to being Prince Raju and Kapi back to being the prince's valet and me back to keeping a safe distance from Dave's feet and bottom, it was time for me and Dave to head home to our shed.

Thinking about our stash of stale bread and our pigeontastic Human Lady waiting for us at home, I couldn't help but think I wouldn't trade our lives for all the silk cushions and golden straw in the world.

I'd definitely trade the Human Lady's Mean Cat for a bowl of mukhwas though.

12
Prince Raju is Off to the Canary Islands

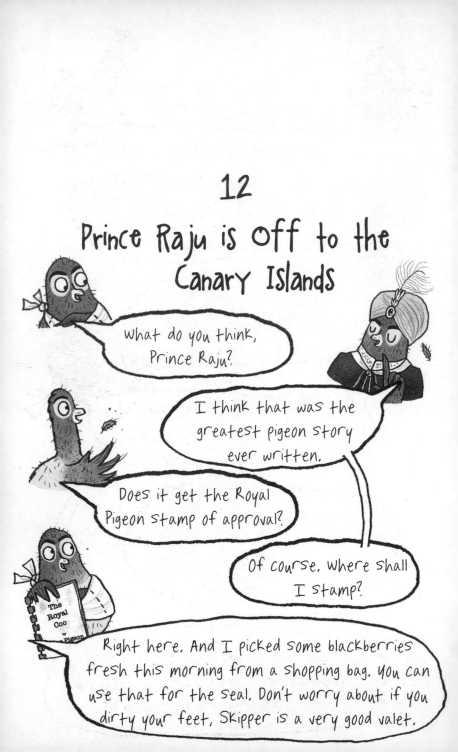

What do you think, Prince Raju?

I think that was the greatest pigeon story ever written.

Does it get the Royal Pigeon stamp of approval?

Of course. Where shall I stamp?

Right here. And I picked some blackberries fresh this morning from a shopping bag. You can use that for the seal. Don't worry about if you dirty your feet, Skipper is a very good valet.

The Real Royal Pigeons

Did you know that the Royal Lofts are based at the Royal Family's home in Sandringham?

That's in Norfolk.

The first ever 'royal pigeons' were given as gifts to the British Royal Human Family by King Leopold II of Belgium over 130 years ago.

That's older than Swapna Haddow who wrote this book and she's REALLY old.

. . . which makes no sense at all. Why would you keep robbers and jewels in the same building?
Some people believe that if the ravens leave the Tower of London, the building will crumble.
That's why there is a Human who makes sure there are six ravens at the tower at all times.
There's a Human who just watches ravens all day long? That's his job?
We call him the Ravenmaster. He feeds us raw meat and bird biscuits, covered in blood. Sometimes we even get to eat an egg, or a bit of rabbit and scraps of fried bread, which is my favourite.

Tinkles and Prince Raju's Guide to the Pigeon Floss

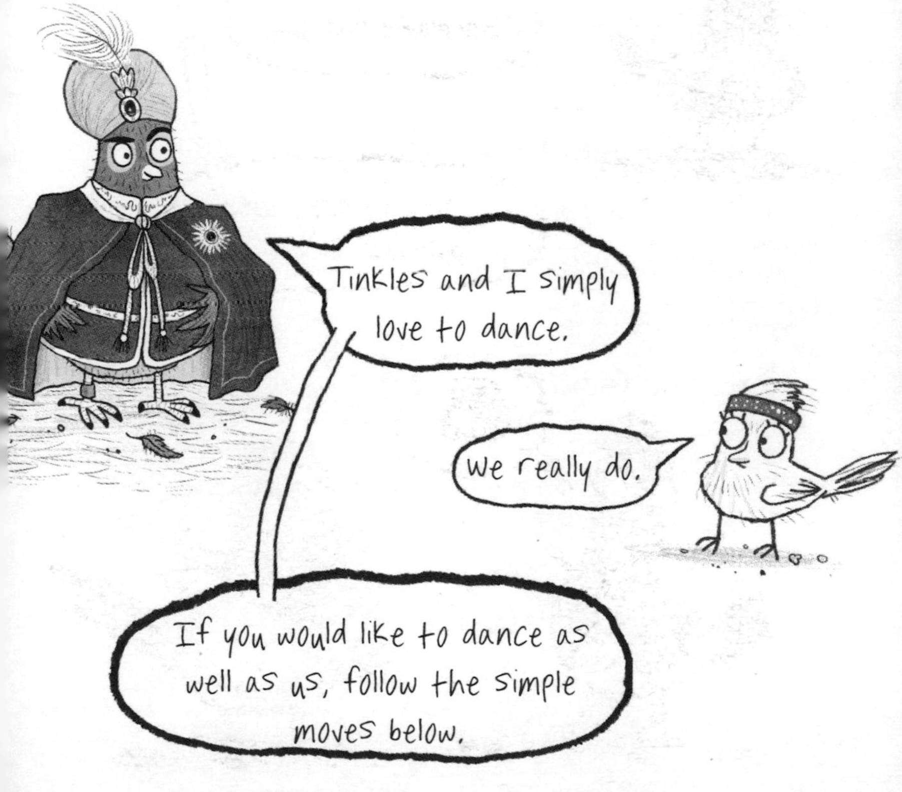

First, you need a claw-tapping beat.

Stand with your legs apart* (but not so far apart you can't get up again).

Swing your wings from left to right (or right to left but not right to right or left to left, that wouldn't make any sense at all).

Now swing those wings around your body whilst moving your tail feathers in the opposite direction.

And you're off!

*backpacks optional

Collect all of Dave and Skipper's adventures . . .

Dave and Skipper's first book where they meet the Human Lady and go on a quest to defeat Mean Cat, the most evil cat in town.

When their Human Lady goes away, Dave and Skipper have to find a new owner. But is Reginald Grimster all he seems? Why is he so keen on feeding them? And why does he have so many books about cooking . . .?

A trip to the pet shop to get Dave's wing fixed leads to a racing competition! Can Dave beat the evil Opprobrious Vastanavius the Parrot?